How Do You Feel?

16 APR 2010

How Do You Feel is designed for adults to share with young children, to help new readers develop early language skills. Children can follow the text as the story is being read to them. If you run your finger under the text as you read, children will learn to read from left to right, and from top to bottom. They should be encouraged to talk about the pictures and to retell the story in their own words.

The words and pictures at the top of the page, which are taken from the story, can be used for discussion, matching and eventually reading. As children's confidence grows, they can begin to pick out initial letter sounds, to read whole words and then phrases for themselves.

The activities at the end will help to develop language skills, to extend vocabulary and reinforce the idea that print and pictures are related and carry meaning.

With special thanks to the children of
Edgware Infant School, London

First published in this edition 2004
By Evans Brothers Limited
2a Portman Mansions
Chiltern Street
London W1U 6NR

Reprinted 2005, twice
© Evans Brothers Ltd 1994
Text copyright © Gillian Liu 1994
Illustrations copyright © Jane Green 1994

Printed in China by WKT Company Limited

ISBN 0 237 52692 1

How Do You Feel?

Written by Gillian Liu
Illustrated by Jane Green

Evans

Evans Brothers Limited

shy   happy   cross   proud   scared

What a busy week! On Monday
I started my new school.

brave   sad   lonely   excited   sleepy

I felt so shy I hid behind daddy's leg!

shy   happy   cross   proud   scared

On Tuesday I met my new friend
Sam and we read lots of books.

brave   sad   lonely   excited   sleepy

I felt so happy I smiled and smiled.

shy   happy   cross   proud   scared

On Wednesday I made a model, but my little sister broke it.

brave   sad   lonely   excited   sleepy

I felt so cross I stamped my feet.

shy   happy   cross   proud   scared

On Thursday I helped my sister
build a model of her own.

I felt so proud I stood up tall.

shy   happy   cross   proud   scared

On Friday I went to the dentist.
I held daddy's hand.

brave   sad   lonely   excited   sleepy

What's the matter?

I feel scared.

I felt so scared my legs were shaking.

shy   happy   cross   proud   scared

The dentist was very kind.
I opened my mouth wide.

brave   sad   lonely   excited   sleepy

I felt very brave.
I grinned and grinned.

shy   happy   cross   proud   scared

On Saturday I lost my teddy.
I felt so sad.

brave   sad   lonely   excited   sleepy

In bed that night I felt so lonely without my teddy.

shy   happy   cross   proud   scared

Today is Sunday. It's my birthday and .... Look what I have found!

brave　　sad　　lonely　　excited　sleepy

I feel so excited.
I want to jump up and down.

brave   sad   lonely   excited   sleepy

Now I feel so sleepy.
It's been a very busy week.

Face puppets

You will need
2 paper plates
1 lollipop stick
felt tip pens
or crayons
wool
glue

1. Put the lollipop stick between the two plates.

2. Stick the two plates together.

3. Draw on the faces - happy on one side, sad on the other side.

4. Stick on wool for the hair.

What other faces can you draw on your plates?

Now you can try to make
face puppets using paper bags.

cross   surprised

Weather chart

Look at the weather every day for a week and make your own weather chart.

March	Sunday	Monday	Tuesday
	rainy	cloudy	sunny
Wednesday	Thursday	Friday	Saturday
windy	snowy	foggy	icy

Now look at your weather chart.

Which day was rainy?

When was it cloudy?

Which day was sunny?

Which day was windy?

Today it is _____.

Yesterday it was _____.

Tomorrow it will be _____.

What would make you happy?

What would make you happy?
What would make you glad?
What would cheer you up,
when you are feeling sad?

I would like to read some books
I would like to read some books
I would like to read some books
That would make me glad.

How Do You Feel is also available as a Big Book
ISBN 0 237 51888 0

For details of this and other books about feelings and emotions,
and teacher resources for PSHE and Citizenship, please contact the
Evans sales department on 020 7487 0920 for a complete catalogue.